FAVOURITE FAIRY TALES

This edition produced exclusively for
Marylebone Books in 1985 by

Octopus Books Limited
59, Grosvenor Street
London W1

ISBN 0 86178 338 7

Design: Design 23

Printed in Yugoslavia

FAVOURITE FAIRY TALES

Translated and adapted by
SUSANNA NOËL

Illustrated by
PAUL DURAND

MARYLEBONE BOOKS

Contents

THE SLEEPING BEAUTY

Once upon a time there lived a king and queen who were very sad because they had no children. They went to all the best doctors and they offered up prayers in all the churches, but with no success. After many years, however, the queen finally gave birth to a daughter, and everyone was overjoyed. The king immediately arranged a splendid banquet and invited all the fairies in the land to be godmothers. Each of the fairies (there were seven of them) was asked to give the baby a special christening gift. After the ceremony the fairies were escorted to the palace, where a grand table had been set out for them. In front of each chair there was a gold dish, and a knife, fork and spoon all wrought from purest gold and decorated with diamonds and rubies.

As they all took their places at the table they saw an old fairy entering the banquet-hall. She had not been invited to the christening because no-one had seen her for fifty years, and the king had thought she was dead or cast under a spell. He immediately asked for a place to be set for her at the table, but he was unable to provide a gold platter because his goldsmiths had made only seven. When she saw this, the old fairy felt insulted and uttered dire threats under her breath. The young fairy sitting next to her listened to her words and, thinking she might be planning to give the little princess an unpleasant christening gift, quickly hid behind a curtain so that she could be the last to speak and in that way repair any harm the old fairy might do.

Meanwhile the fairies had begun to give their presents to the baby. The first fairy said that she would be the most beautiful baby in all the world, the second that she would have the spirit of an angel, the third that her every action would be filled with grace, the fourth that she would dance beautifully, the fifth that she would have the voice of a nightingale, and the sixth that she would be able to play every kind of musical instrument.

Then came the turn of the old fairy, who, shaking her head in anger, said that the princess would prick her finger on a needle and die. A gasp went through the company when they heard these words, and many of the courtiers shed a tear at the thought of the baby's fate.

At that moment, the young fairy who had hidden behind the curtain stood up before them all and spoke the following words:

'Be consoled, your Majesties, your daughter will not die; although I do not have the power to undo the old fairy's gift completely, I can make it a little easier for you. The princess will prick her finger on a needle, but instead of dying, she will fall into a deep, deep sleep that will last for a hundred years. She will sleep until she is awakened by a king's son.'

The king, hoping to avoid the misfortune predicted by the wicked fairy, forbade everyone in the kingdom to sew with a spindle-wheel.

When the princess was fifteen or sixteen years old, the king and queen took her with them to their summer castle. One day, the princess was exploring the upper rooms of the castle, and she climbed to the top of a small tower where she found an old woman sitting in a garret sewing with a spindle. This good woman did not know that the king had forbidden people to have spindles on pain of death.

'What is that you are doing?' asked the princess.

'Why, I'm sewing, child,' replied the old lady.

'Oh, it is pretty!' cried the princess. 'How do you do it? Let me see if I can do it too!' and she tried to grab hold of the needle.

It pricked her finger and she fell in a faint on the ground. The old woman was very upset and called for help. Servants ran from all parts of the palace and gathered round the princess, splashing her face with water and unlacing her bodice to try and revive her. But she lay quite still.

The king, hearing all the noise, rushed up to the tower and saw that the wicked fairy's prediction had come true. Sadly he told his servants to lay the princess to rest in the most beautiful room in the palace, on a bed made of silver and wrought gold.

Her eyes were closed, but she was not dead because she was breathing gently. The king ordered everyone to leave her in peace until the time came for her to be awakened by a prince.

The good fairy who had been the last to speak at the christening was a thousand miles away when the accident happened, but a little dwarf told her about it and she set off immediately for the palace, riding in a chariot of fire drawn by two dragons. The good fairy felt it might be a bit lonely for the princess when she woke up in a hundred years' time in an empty old castle, so this is what she did:

She touched everyone in the castle with her wand except the king and queen, and she also touched all the animals including the princess's dog, who was lying beside her on the bed. As she touched them they fell asleep one by one, not to wake up for a hundred years; even the partridges and pheasants that were sizzling on the fire fell asleep, and so did the fire itself. All this happened in a twinkling of an eye because fairies never waste time.

Then the king and queen left the palace, and in the space of half-an-hour a thick forest of tall trees had grown around the castle, surrounded by a thorny hedge with prickles. It was impossible for anyone to get through.

After a hundred years had gone by, the son of a neighbouring king was riding past the thorny forest on his way home from hunting, and he asked one of his companions what the towers could be. One of them told him it must be a haunted castle; another one said he had heard that wizards held their meetings there. But most people thought that it was the home of a wicked ogre, who kidnapped children and took them back there to gobble up when he got hungry. They said that no-one could follow him, because he was the only one who knew the way through the thorny forest.

The prince didn't know which of these stories to believe, but then an old peasant spoke up:

'Your Highness, more than fifty years ago I remember my father talking about a beautiful princess who was cast under a spell that would make her sleep for a hundred years, until she was awakened by the son of a king, and I think that is the castle she was living in when she fell asleep.'

The young prince was filled with curiosity at this, and decided that he would try and make his way to the castle. He fought his way through the thorns and prickles until he could see the castle at the end of a long avenue. To his surprise, none of his companions had been able to follow him, because the trees and hedges had closed in behind him. Bravely he walked down the road and entered a huge courtyard, where a scene met his eyes that made him shiver with fear.

It looked as if everyone in the castle were dead, but when he looked more closely he could see that their faces were still rosy with health and they were all breathing gently. He walked through the courtyard and up a staircase where the guards stood asleep at their posts, with their rifles on their shoulders. He passed through several rooms filled with ladies-in-waiting and gentlemen of the court, all of them asleep, some standing, some seated. He then went into a room which was painted in gold, and there lying on a bed he saw the most beautiful girl he had ever set eyes on, a radiant expression on her lovely face. Trembling, he went up to the bed and knelt beside it, and kissed her cheek. The princess stretched her arms, opened her eyes and smiled at him, her eyes tender with love.

'Is it you, my prince?' she asked.

Enchanted by her words, the young prince declared his love for her and asked her to be his wife.

The princess put on her most beautiful dress and all her jewels. Then she and the prince went downstairs to the dining-hall and had a huge feast served by the footmen of the castle.

Up in the music gallery, minstrels played music that had not been heard for a hundred years, and everyone danced and sang and laughed for joy.

A few days later the prince and princess were married and lived happily together for many more years.

CINDERELLA

Once upon a time there lived a nobleman whose second wife was the proudest and haughtiest creature you ever did see. She had two ugly daughters who resembled her in every way, while for his part the nobleman had a little daughter who had inherited all the good qualities of her own dead mother. No sooner were the wedding celebrations over and done with than the step-mother began to make changes in the household.

She found that her step-daughter's sweet and gentle nature only made her own two daughters even more disagreeable by comparison, so she made the young girl do all the horrid jobs around the house and forbade her to leave the kitchen when her work was done.

The young step-daughter had to sleep in a tiny attic right at the top of the house on a lumpy old straw mattress, while her sisters slept in magnificent rooms with parquet floors, enormous feather-beds and looking-glasses that reached from the floor to the ceiling. The poor girl suffered it all in silence, and did not dare to complain to her father, who would only have scolded her anyway, because he was entirely under her stepmother's thumb. When her work was done, she would go to the fireplace where the cinders were still glowing, and try to keep herself warm. Because the ugly sisters always found her there in the evenings, they used to call her Cinderella.

However although Cinderella dressed in rags and tatters, she was far more beautiful than her sisters and they were jealous of her.

One day the king's son decided to give a grand ball, and invited everybody of importance to it. This meant that even the ugly sisters were invited, and they immediately set about choosing their ball-gowns. The older sister said, 'I'm going to wear my red velvet dress with the white ruffles, and with it I'm going to wear my diamond tiara.'

'Well, my dress may not be as fancy as yours,' retorted the younger sister, 'but I'm going to wear my emerald necklace, and *that* will outshine you, sister dear! Cinderella! Come here at once and tell me if my emeralds aren't far finer than my sister's diamonds!'

Cinderella came running, and gave her opinion, which in spite of themselves they valued, because she had good taste. She offered to dress their hair for them, and they were delighted, because her fingers were deft and skilful. As she was combing the elder sister's hair, they asked her, 'Well, Cinders, surely you're going to the ball?'

'Don't mock me, sisters,' said Cinderella sadly. 'You know I can't go to the ball! I have no fine dress and jewels.'

'You're absolutely right,' retorted the older sister. 'People would split their sides laughing if you turned up!'

Someone more malicious than Cinderella might have washed their hair in coal-tar but she had a good heart and dressed their hair beautifully. The sisters had not eaten for nearly three days so that they would be able to squeeze into their ball-dresses, and even then Cinderella had to lace them into their corsets by pulling on the bedposts.

Finally they left and Cinderella watched them through the window until they were tiny specks in the distance. When she could see them no longer, she sat down and cried. Suddenly her beautiful fairy godmother appeared!

'You want to go to the prince's ball, don't you, my dear?' she said.

'Oh, yes,' sobbed Cinderella.

'Well, you *shall* go,' said the fairy godmother. 'Do just as I say! First of all, go into the garden and bring me a pumpkin.'

Cinderella picked the finest pumpkin she could see and carried it to her godmother, quite puzzled as to how a pumpkin was going to get her to the palace. Her fairy godmother waved her wand over the pumpkin and then tapped it three times. It changed into a beautiful carriage!

Then the fairy godmother found the kitchen mousetrap, which had six squealing mice in it. She told Cinderella to lift the door of the trap and let the mice out one by one. As they came out she tapped each of them on the head with her wand and changed it into a prancing horse. Soon there was a team of six dapple-grey horses, and she began to look round for something to turn into a coachman.

'Shall I go and see if there are any rats in the rat-hole?' asked Cinderella.

'Yes, child,' said the godmother. 'Bring the largest and fattest one to me.'

Cinderella chose the rat with the longest whiskers and her godmother tapped it on the head with her wand. It turned into a big fat coachman with an enormous moustache.

Then she turned to Cinderella and said, 'See if you can find six lizards out in the garden.' No sooner had Cinderella brought six lizards into the house than the fairy godmother tapped them each on the head and six footmen stood before them, all dressed in splendid uniforms. 'There you are, child!' said the godmother triumphantly. 'Now you can go to the ball!'

'But, godmother,' said Cinderella sadly, 'how can I go in these dirty old rags?'

Then her fairy godmother tapped Cinderella with her wand. Cinderella suddenly found she was wearing a beautiful silk ball-dress embroidered with precious stones, and a pair of delicate glass slippers.

She gasped with pleasure, and hugged her godmother for joy. But as she climbed into the carriage, her godmother said, 'Now, do not stay a minute later than midnight, child! On the stroke of twelve your carriage will turn back into a pumpkin, your horses will become mice again, and you will find yourself dressed in rags.'

Cinderella promised her godmother that she would leave the ball on the stroke of midnight, and set off for the palace.

As she drove up to the palace gates, the courtiers ran and told the prince that a beautiful unknown princess had arrived, and he came to greet her. He helped her down from the carriage and led her into the ballroom.

As they entered the violins stopped playing, the dancing came to a halt and everybody stopped talking, as they all stared in wonder at the beauty of this unknown princess! A murmur went through the crowd, 'Oh, how lovely she is!' 'Did you ever see anyone so beautiful?' Even the king himself, old as he was, could not take his eyes off her, and whispered to the queen, 'It's years and years since I've seen anyone so pretty!'

The prince seated her in the place of honour and then invited her to dance. Her dancing was so graceful that everyone admired her even more. Then a splendid banquet was served, but the prince could not eat anything because he was so busy looking at Cinderella. For a time she even sat next to her sisters and gave them some of the sweetmeats that the prince kept pressing her to take. This astonished them considerably because they did not recognise her at all.

Suddenly Cinderella heard the clock striking a quarter to midnight, and she immediately made a graceful bow to the assembled company and ran towards the gates where her carriage was waiting. As soon as she got back home, she thanked her godmother, and asked if she could go to the ball again the following evening.

Just as she was in the middle of telling her fairy godmother about everything that had happened, she heard her sisters knocking at the door and hurried to open it.

'What a long time you've been!' she said, rubbing her eyes and pretending that she had only just woken up.

'Oh, we had such a wonderful time!' said the older sister. 'There was the most beautiful princess you have ever seen. She was charming to us, and look, she gave us candied oranges!'

Cinderella could hardly contain her joy and she asked the name of the lovely princess. The ugly sisters said that nobody knew it and that she was a mystery.

'The young prince is madly in love with her,' said the younger sister. 'He says he would give anything in the world to know who she is!' Cinderella smiled and said, 'Was she really so beautiful? How lucky you are! I wish I could see her just once! Do you suppose I could borrow one of your dresses, just an everyday one?'

'What an idea!' said the sisters indignantly. 'What impertinence! Lend a grubby little thing like you one of our fine dresses? You must think we're mad!'

Cinderella expected this response and, to be truthful, she was not worried by it because she would not have wanted to wear one of their cast-off dresses.

The next day, the sisters set off for the palace, and as soon as they had gone the fairy godmother waved her wand and Cinderella followed them in her carriage. The prince was overjoyed to see her again and never left her side for a moment. Cinderella had such a happy time that she completely forgot what her godmother had said. Time flew by, and when she heard the stroke of twelve she jumped up and ran as fast as she could down the stairs from the palace.

As she ran down the long staircase, Cinderella dropped one of her glass slippers. Her dress turned back to rags and the carriage disappeared.

Fortunately the prince was too far away to see. All he found was the little glass slipper, and this he kept safe, determined to find its owner.

The only thing that remained with Cinderella of all her finery was the other little glass slipper; the pair to the one the prince found.

When the ugly sisters got back from the ball, Cinderella asked
them if they had enjoyed themselves, and if the beautiful princess
had been there. They replied that she had, but she had run away
just as midnight struck, leaving behind a little glass slipper, which
the prince had picked up and put in his pocket. They said he kept
kissing it all evening, and they were sure he was in love with the
mysterious beauty.

A few days later the palace made an announcement that the prince would marry the girl whose foot fitted the glass slipper. First of all the princesses of the court tried the slipper on, then the duchesses, and then all the rest of the court, but not one of them could get it on. Finally it was brought to the ugly sisters, who did everything they could to force their big fat feet into the tiny little slipper, but it was no good at all.

Cinderella was watching them and of course she recognised the slipper immediately. Timidly she asked, 'Do you think I could try it on?'

The ugly sisters hooted with rude laughter, but the nobleman who had brought the slipper looked attentively at Cinderella and found her very pretty. He told the ugly sisters that he had orders from the prince to let every girl in the kingdom try the slipper on. He made Cinderella sit down in front of him, and then slid the slipper on to her foot. It fitted like a kid glove!

The ugly sisters were even more astonished when Cinderella took out the other matching slipper and put it on her other foot. Just then her fairy godmother appeared and tapped Cinderella's clothes with her wand. Once more she was dressed in a beautiful gown.

Immediately the ugly sisters recognised her as the beautiful princess they had seen at the ball. They threw themselves at her feet and asked her to forgive them for all their unkind acts and bad treatment.

Cinderella told them to stand up, and kissed them both, saying that she forgave them and would always love them. Then she was taken to the prince, who found her more beautiful then ever, and a few days later they were married. Cinderella, who was as good as she was beautiful, invited her sisters to live with her in the palace and within a short time they were both married to two noblemen of the court.

TOM
THUMB

Once upon a time there lived a woodcutter and his wife who had seven children, all of them boys. The oldest was not yet ten, while the youngest was already seven years old. Everyone was amazed that they had so many children in so short a time, but the woodcutter's wife always seemed to have two babies at once. They were very poor, and found it difficult to make ends meet with such a large family, particularly because the boys were not yet old enough to earn their own living.

What made them even more unhappy was the fact that their youngest child had never spoken a word. He was very small, and in fact when he was born he was no bigger than a man's thumb, so they nicknamed him Tom Thumb. This child was the bane of their life and caused them a lot of grief. However, if the truth were told he was the wisest of all his brothers, and because he didn't say anything he had plenty of time to listen and learn.

One year the winter was very severe, and no one had any food. One evening, after the boys were all in bed, the woodcutter said to his wife, 'My dear, we have nothing to give our children to eat. I can't bear to watch them dying of hunger in front of our eyes, so I have decided to take them into the middle of the forest to fend for themselves. While they are gathering wood, we will run away without them noticing us.'

'Oh, husband!' cried the woodcutter's wife. 'Surely you can't mean what you say? We can't lose our children!' She knew they were poor, but she was their mother, and she couldn't bear the thought of losing them. After a while, though, she realised how painful it would be to watch her children die of hunger, so she agreed to do what her husband planned and then cried herself to sleep.

Tom Thumb had been hiding under their bed, so he had heard every word. He crept silently back to his own bed, but didn't sleep a wink all night for worrying about what would happen to him and his brothers. He didn't say anything to them about what he had heard, but early the next morning he got up quietly and went down to the stream to fill his pockets with tiny white pebbles.

Then he went back to the woodcutter's house, and in due course they all set off into the forest. They had to walk in single file because the trees were so close together that two people could not walk abreast. The woodcutter began cutting down trees, and all the boys began collecting firewood. When the woodcutter and his wife saw that the boys were occupied in their work, they moved quietly away and suddenly disappeared down a narrow path.

When the boys realized they had been left alone, they began to cry. Tom Thumb didn't cry, because he knew how he would be able

to get back home. As he had walked along, he had dropped a trail
of the little white pebbles he had picked up on the banks of the
stream. So he said, 'Don't worry, brothers! Father and mother have
left us here, but I know how to get us back home. Follow me!' So
they followed him and he led them back to the woodcutter's hut.
At first they didn't dare to go in, but hid behind the door to hear
what their parents were saying.

58

At the very moment that the woodcutter and his wife had returned home, the squire of the village had paid them ten pieces of gold that he had owed them for a long time and which they had given up for lost. This gave them hope because they were dying of hunger. The woodcutter sent his wife to the butcher's to buy meat, and since she hadn't eaten for a very long time she bought three times as much meat as was needed to make soup for two people.

When they had eaten their fill, the woodcutter's wife said, 'Alas, where are our poor sons now? They were so dear to me! But it's you, William, who wanted to take them into the forest. I knew we would regret it. What can they be doing, lost as they are? Oh, dear God, I hope they haven't been eaten by wolves. How unkind it was of you to want to lose your children in this way!'

At length the woodcutter grew impatient, because she had said twenty times over that they would regret it and that it was his fault. He threatened to beat her, so she kept quiet, but she could not keep back her tears, and from time to time she would say, 'Alas, alas, where are my poor children now?' Finally she said it so loudly that the children hiding behind the door couldn't keep quiet any longer, and shouted, 'Here we are, here we are!'

She ran quickly to open the door, and hugged and kissed them, saying, 'Oh, how happy I am to see you, my dear children! You must be dying of hunger, and Peter, how dirty you are! Come here and let me wash your face!' (Peter was her favourite son.)

Then they all sat down at table and ate with enormous appetites which gave their parents a lot of pleasure, and they told their parents what they had seen and done in the forest, all of them talking at once. The good woodcutter and his wife were overjoyed to have their children back, and their joy lasted as long as the gold pieces lasted.

However, when the money ran out they fell into despair and decided to take the children into the forest again, this time much further – so that they would not be able to find their way back home. Tom Thumb again overheard his parents' plans, and planned to do the same as he had done before. He got up early the next morning to go and collect more pebbles but he couldn't get out of the house because the kitchen door was bolted right at the top, and he couldn't reach it. He could not get out, so when his mother gave each of the boys a crust of bread for their lunch, he decided to break it up into crumbs and save them. The woodcutter and his wife led the boys into the densest part of the forest and then left them, as before.

Tom Thumb was not worried, because he had left a trail of crumbs to lead them safely back home. Imagine his dismay when he saw that the birds had followed behind them and eaten all the crumbs up! The boys were in despair, because the further they walked the more they got lost. Night fell, and there was a great wind which howled around them and frightened them all very much. It sounded as though they were surrounded by a pack of fierce wolves that was about to come and eat them up. The boys all sat perfectly still, not daring even to move their heads. Then it began to rain and in no time at all they were drenched to the bone; they slipped and slid in the mud and each of them fell over several times.

Tom Thumb climbed up a tall tree and far off in the distance he could see a dim light like a candle. He climbed down again and led his brothers in the direction of the light, and after walking for a long time they came to the edge of the forest and saw a house in front of them. They knocked at the door, and a woman with a good-

natured face opened it. They explained that they had got lost in the forest, and begged the good woman to give them shelter. At this she burst into tears and said, 'Oh, children, you shouldn't have come here! Do you know whose house this is? It's the home of a wicked ogre who eats little children for breakfast, lunch and dinner!'

'Oh dear, oh dear!' cried Tom Thumb, trembling from head to foot. 'What shall we do? If you don't give us a place for the night, the wolves in the forest will certainly eat us up! And if that's the case, we would prefer to be eaten by the ogre because, who knows, he might take pity on us if you beg him to.'

The ogre's wife, who thought she might be able to hide them until the following morning, let them come in and warm themselves by the fire. She gave them some pieces of the sheep that was roasting on a spit for the ogre's dinner. Just as they were beginning to warm up, they heard a great knocking at the door. 'Quickly, children!' said the ogre's wife. 'It's my husband. Come here and hide under the bed!' Then she went to the door and let her husband in. The

ogre asked in a loud, gruff voice if dinner was ready, and told his wife to fetch him a jug of wine. Then he sat down at the table. The roast mutton was still dripping with blood, but the ogre smacked his lips and said he had never eaten better. Then he began to turn this way and that, saying, 'I smell raw meat! I smell raw meat!'

'Nonsense!' said his wife, 'it must be this calf that I've just killed for your breakfast.'

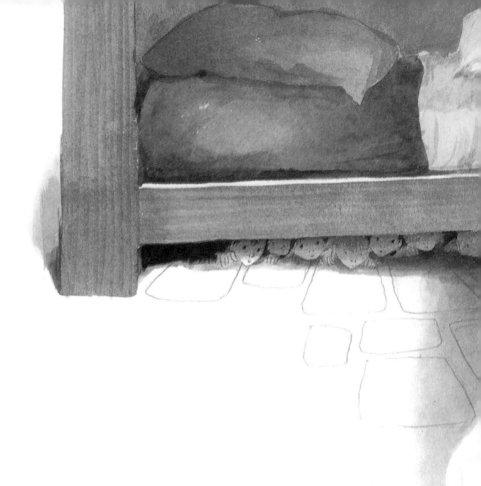

'I tell you, I smell raw meat!' repeated the ogre, squinting at his wife. 'There's something in this room that's good for ogres to eat.' As he spoke these words he got up from the table and went over to the bed. 'Aha, you wicked woman!' he shouted. 'You have deceived me! If you weren't so old and tough I'd eat you on the spot! As it is, these tasty little morsels will make a treat for me and three of my friends.'

He dragged the boys out from under the bed one by one. The poor children begged him on their knees not to eat them, but he was the most cruel of all the ogres, and far from taking pity on them he would have gobbled them up then and there but for the fact that there wasn't any gravy to go with them. He told his wife to make the sauce and he went to fetch his big carving-knife, which he sharpened on a flintstone. He had just picked up the oldest of the boys by the hair when his wife said, 'What good will that do at this hour of night? All your friends will have had their dinner! Far better to wait until tomorrow and have a proper dinner-party!'

'I suppose you're right,' said the ogre. 'Well then, give them some supper to fatten them all up a bit and then put them to bed.' The good wife was delighted at his words, and brought the boys a hearty supper, but they could not eat a bite, because they were so frightened. As for the ogre, he was well satisfied with the prospect of entertaining his friends on such tempting morsels, and drank a couple of jugs of wine to celebrate. He drank considerably more than usual, and the wine went to his head a little, so he stumbled off to bed.

The ogre had seven daughters, who were still quite young. They all had wonderful complexions because, like their father, they ate a lot of raw meat, but they had little round eyes and crooked noses, and huge mouths with sharp, pointed teeth. They had all been put to bed early, and all seven of them were fast asleep in a big bed, with gold crowns on their heads. There was another bed in the same room, and it was in this bed that the ogre's wife put the seven

boys to sleep. Then she went to sleep next to her husband. Tom Thumb noticed that the daughters all slept with crowns on. He was a bit worried in case the ogre got up in the night feeling hungry so he got up quietly and tiptoed across to the bed where the ogre's daughters lay sleeping. Gently he took their crowns off their heads. Instead he put seven nightcaps on their heads and then crept back to his brothers and put the seven crowns on their heads. Sure enough, just as he had feared, the ogre was woken up by his stomach rumbling, and remembered the tasty morsels lying in the next room.

He got unsteadily out of bed, picked up his big knife and set off on tiptoe up the stairs. 'They won't get off a second time,' he muttered to himself. 'This time they're for it! I'm too hungry!'

He went into the big bedroom and went towards the bed he thought the boys were sleeping in. He was just about to raise his knife when he noticed the crowns on their heads. 'Good heavens, I must have drunk a bit too much! I've come to the wrong bed!' he said, and went over to the bed where all his daughters were fast asleep wearing nightcaps. 'Aha!' said the ogre. 'Here they are.' And he chopped up his daughters by mistake. He then felt he had to go and lie down again, and stumbled down the stairs back to his bed.

As soon as Tom Thumb was sure the ogre had gone back to sleep, he awoke his brothers and told them to dress quickly and follow him. They went quietly down into the garden and climbed over the wall. They ran nearly all night, trembling with fear and not really knowing where they were going. The next morning, when the ogre woke up he said to his wife: 'Go and dress those tasty little morsels for my dinner!' His wife thought he meant her to put the boys' clothes on for them, not realizing that he meant her to cook them. She went up the stairs and discovered the remains of her seven daughters, She was so horrified she fainted dead away.

The ogre, getting impatient, went upstairs to see what was keeping her so long. He was no less astonished than his wife at the sight that met his eyes. 'Oh, goodness, what have I done?' he cried. 'I'll catch those little varmints yet, so I will!'

He threw a bucket of water over his wife's head to revive her, and said to her, 'Find me my seven-league boots! I'm going to find those boys!' He set off immediately and in no time at all he saw the seven boys trudging wearily along. In fact they were only a hundred yards from their parents' house, but they didn't know it. They looked back and saw the ogre leaping from mountain to mountain and crossing rivers in a single bound, and Tom Thumb quickly hid himself and his brothers under a big rock.

It just so happened that the ogre, who was tired after his long journey, decided to sit down on the rock and rest himself. In a short while he fell fast asleep and began to snore so thunderously that the boys were even more terrified than they had been when he had been standing over them with a carving-knife. Tom Thumb managed to keep his head, and told his brothers to run away while the ogre was still asleep. They took his advice, and all of them reached their parents' house safe and sound.

74

Tom Thumb, who had stayed behind, bravely went up to the giant and took off his seven-league boots. Then he put them on himself, and because they were fairy-boots they fitted Tom Thumb perfectly. (They had the ability to make the person who wore them as large as they were!) Tom Thumb set off immediately for the ogre's house, where he found the good wife still weeping over the loss of her daughters.

'Your husband is in grave danger,' said Tom Thumb. 'He has been taken prisoner by a gang of thieves who have threatened to kill him unless he gives them all his silver and gold. Just as they were about to slit his throat, he saw me and begged me to come and ask you to give me all his valuables, otherwise the thieves will have no mercy on him and will kill him. Because it's very urgent, he has lent me·his seven-league boots.'

The poor wife, not knowing what to do, handed over everything she possessed to Tom Thumb, because she was fond of her husband even though he did have the nasty habit of eating small children. Tom Thumb, loaded up with all the ogre's riches, set off home, where he was received with great rejoicing. The woodcutter and his wife were able to buy a splendid new house and all the other things they needed, and none of them, thanks to Tom Thumb, ever went hungry again.

PUSS
IN
BOOTS

There was once an honest miller who died and left all he had to his three sons. The oldest son inherited his mill, the middle son inherited his donkey, and the youngest inherited his cat, for those were the only things the poor miller possessed. The youngest sat under a tree bemoaning his lot. 'My brothers have the chance to earn their living honestly, with the mill and the donkey, but as for me, once I have eaten the cat and made myself a coat out of its fur, I will go cold and hungry.' The cat, hearing these words, said to him in a serious tone of voice (for he didn't at all fancy being made into a fur coat):

'Don't upset yourself, master! Just give me a sack, and make me a pair of boots so that I can get through the undergrowth, and you will see that you have not been so badly done to after all.'

Although the youngest son did not place any great hopes on the cat's abilities, he had seen the speed and cunning with which he caught rats and mice and the agility with which he escaped from the neighbourhood dog, so he thought there might be some hope of being rescued from his misery. When the cat had his boots, he put his sack on his back and set off for a wood where he knew there were lots of rabbits. He put the sack on the ground with some carrots sticking out of it, and then hid behind a tree. He had barely had time to hide when a little rabbit came bounding towards the sack, eager to see what was in it. As soon as the rabbit's head was inside, Puss-in-Boots pulled the strings of the sack as hard as he could and trapped it.

Then he went to the palace and demanded to see the king. Standing in front of the throne, he said, 'Your Majesty, in this sack I have a rabbit which my master, the Marquis of Caracas, has asked me to give to you personally.'

'Tell your master I am very grateful to him, and shall enjoy eating it,' said the king graciously.

The following day, Puss-in-Boots went into a field of barley and left his sack in the middle of it with the neck open. Then he lay down beside it and pretended to be dead. After a short time, two fat partridges waddled up to the sack and put their heads into it, and quick as a flash Puss-in-Boots pulled the strings tight and trapped them. The king was even more delighted with the partridges, and gave the cat a gold coin.

Over the next few months, Puss-in-Boots continued to take the king delicacies that he managed to catch here and there. Then one day, when he knew the king would be driving along the river-bank with his beautiful daughter, Puss-in-Boots said to his master, 'If you follow my advice, your fortune will be made. All you have to do is to go swimming in the river at a place I will take you to, and leave the rest to me.'

The Marquis of Caracas did as he was told, without knowing what his cat had in mind. While he was bathing in the river, the king drove past in his coach, and Puss-in-Boots immediately began shouting at the top of his voice, 'Help! Help! My master the Marquis of Caracas is drowning!'

When the king heard all the shouting, he put his head out of the window of the coach and recognised the cat who had brought him so many good things to eat. He ordered his officers to go to the aid of the Marquis of Caracas. While they were pulling the poor marquis out of the river, the cat went up to the coach and told the king that while his master was bathing some thieves had stolen all his clothes, even though he had shouted, 'Stop, thief!' at the top of his voice. The king immediately ordered his gentlemen of the wardrobe to bring one of his finest robes for the young marquis to put on.

Once dressed in the splendid robes, the young marquis really looked very handsome, and the king was quite taken with him. It

has to be said that the king's beautiful daughter also found him to her liking. The marquis had only to give her one or two tender glances and she fell madly in love with him. The king invited him to come for a ride with them in the coach.

Delighted at the success of his plan, the cat took the initiative and told some peasants who were tilling a field that it belonged to his master the Marquis of Caracas.

'In a few minutes the king will drive past in his coach, and if you don't tell him that the field belongs to the Marquis of Caracas, I will come and cut you into little pieces.' As the king drove past, he leant out of the window and asked, 'My good fellows, who does this large field belong to?' They all replied at once, 'Why, your Majesty, it belongs to the famous Marquis of Caracas!'

'Ah, you own land in this area, do you?' said the king.

'As you see, Sire,' replied the marquis. 'I have several fields, all of which give a good harvest every year.'

Meanwhile, Puss-in-Boots had run on ahead again, and saw some peasants harvesting corn. 'My men!' he shouted in a loud voice, 'the king is going to ride past in a minute or two, and if you don't tell him that this corn belongs to the Marquis of Caracas I personally will come and cut you into little pieces.'

And sure enough, as the king drove past he wanted to know who the corn belonged to. 'Why, it belongs to the famous Marquis of Caracas, Sire!' replied the harvesters in unison, and the king was even more impressed.

Puss-in-Boots went ahead of the carriage telling everyone what to say and the king was astonished at the great possessions of the Marquis of Caracas. Finally Puss-in-Boots arrived at a castle where there lived a fierce ogre, the richest ogre in the world, because in fact all the lands that the king had passed through on his ride belonged to him.

The cat wanted to know who the ogre was, and so he demanded to talk to him, saying that he didn't want to pass by so close to the castle without paying his respects to its owner. The ogre greeted him as politely as an ogre can, and invited him to take a seat.

'I have heard that you can turn yourself into all kinds of animals,' said the cat in a conversational tone. 'For instance, can you turn yourself into a lion, or an elephant?'

'I certainly can,' replied the ogre abruptly, 'and to prove it I'll turn myself into a lion for you.' The cat was so frightened at seeing a roaring lion in front of him that he leapt for the roof, not without difficulty because his boots were no good for walking on tiles.

When he saw that the ogre had returned to his normal appearance, Puss-in-Boots climbed down again, saying he had been quite scared. 'I'm also told,' said Puss, 'that you can turn yourself into all sorts of little animals – rats and mice, for example. But I'm not sure I believe that, because you are so large. It seems impossible to me!'

'Impossible, eh?' growled the ogre. 'Impossible indeed! I'll show you!' and in a trice he turned himself into a mouse and began running across the floor. No sooner had he done this than Puss jumped down and gobbled the mouse up. Just at that moment the king drove past the castle and decided he wanted to stop and find out who lived in it. Puss-in-Boots, hearing the noise of carriage-wheels crossing the drawbridge, ran out and said to the king, 'Welcome to the castle of my master the Marquis of Caracas!'

'Dear me!' exclaimed the king, 'does this castle belong to him as well?' He turned to the young marquis and said, 'I would be **much** obliged if you would show us round.' The marquis gave his hand to the young princess, and followed the king into a huge room where they found a table set with a magnificent banquet that the ogre had ordered for himself. The king, already delighted with the qualities of the Marquis of Caracas, was no less charmed by his obvious wealth and possessions, and, seeing that his daughter was madly in love with the young man, he said to him after five or six glasses of wine, 'Well, my boy, it looks as though you are going to be my son-in-law!'

The marquis made a low bow and accepted the honour gratefully, and the following day he and the princess were married. Puss-in-Boots was made a lord, and now no longer has to catch mice except for his own amusement.

LITTLE DONKEY SKIN

Once upon a time there lived a king who was so great and so beloved by his subjects that he was the happiest of rulers. He had a wife who was as beautiful as she was good, and they lived together in a beautiful palace. They had one daughter, who was so charming and graceful that they did not regret the fact that she was their only child.

The king had the best stables in the kingdom, filled with beautiful horses, but everyone who went to see them was amazed that the best stable of all was occupied by a long-eared donkey. The king had given orders for the donkey to have a special place in the stables because it had a magical gift. Every morning, the floor of its stall was covered by gold pieces, which the stable-boys would collect when they came to feed him.

Now, since good luck and bad luck are always mixed, and bad luck falls on the shoulders of kings and their loyal subjects alike, the queen one day became very ill, and no one could find a cure, not even the wisest of the king's doctors. Everyone in the kingdom was overcome with sadness. The king, who loved his wife very dearly, was very distressed and prayed to all the gods, offering them his life if they would save his wife, but his prayers were not heard. The queen, on her deathbed, said to her weeping husband:

'Before I die, I have one last thing to ask you. Please get married again!'

At these words the king began to cry even more, and bent his head over his wife's hands.

'No, no, my darling queen!' he cried, 'I cannot marry again. I would rather follow you!'

'That you must not do,' replied the queen with a firmness that made the king's heart sink. 'You need an heir, a son who can take the throne when you die; so you must find another wife. But one thing I would like you to promise me, if you really love me. Don't marry unless you find a princess who is more beautiful than I am! If I can have your word of honour about that, I will die happy.'

It is possible that the queen made this demand because she felt sure that there was no woman in the kingdom as beautiful as she was, and that therefore her husband would never re-marry. Finally she breathed her last breath, and the king was distressed for many weeks, crying day and night.

But all sorrow comes to an end, and one day, seeing that he was beginning to recover, the dukes and earls of the kingdom came to the king and begged him to marry again. The very suggestion made him burst into tears, and he reminded them of the promise he had given the queen. He told them to go and look for a princess who was more beautiful than his wife had been. But his noblemen told him that beauty was not important provided that a queen was virtuous and produced heirs to the throne. He must have an heir so that the peace and tranquility of the kingdom could be secured. Although the young princess was good and beautiful, she would have to marry a prince from another kingdom, who would then take her back home with him. Even if her husband chose to remain and rule with her, their children would be of his blood, and the neighbouring kingdoms might use this as an excuse to start wars against them. The king was struck by these comments, and promised to reflect upon them.

So he began to look for a new wife. Every day his courtiers brought him portraits of charming girls, but not one of them was as beautiful as his wife had been. He began to realize more and more that his daughter was the only girl in the land who was more lovely than her mother had been. Her freshness and youth filled the king with such a violent love that he could not hide it from thc princess and told her that she was his choice for a second wife, since she was the only woman who could release him from his promise. The young princess nearly fainted when she heard these words. She threw herself at her father's feet and begged him not to make her commit such a terrible crime.

The king, who had this idea now firmly in his head, went to his head priest and told him to calm the fears of the young princess. The priest sacrificed the innocence of the king's daughter by telling her that it would not be a crime for the king to marry his own daughter. The king embraced him and returned home more obsessed than before with his project. He gave orders for the princess to obey him.

The young princess, in great distress, decided to seek advice from her godmother, the fairy Lilac, and set off that same night in a carriage drawn by a large sheep who knew the way to Fairyland. She arrived there the next day. Lilac, who loved the little princess, said she already knew everything about the king's plans, but that the princess need have no worries. Nothing could harm her if she followed faithfully the instructions she was about to give her. 'My dear child,' she said, 'it would be a great sin to marry your father; but you can escape doing so without angering him if you do as I tell you. Go and ask your father for a dress the colour of the sky. I'm quite sure he won't be able to find anyone who can make one for him.'

The princess thanked her godmother, and the following morning she did as the fairy had advised her and told the king that she would only consent to marry him if he gave her a dress that was the colour of the sky. The king, delighted by this ray of hope, called together the most famous tailors in the land and commanded them to make a dress that was the colour of the sky, saying that if they did not succeed they would all be hanged. Two days later the tailors brought him the dress.

The sky when it is filled with golden clouds could not be so beautiful as the dress that they spread out in front of the king and his daughter. The princess was dismayed, and did not know what to do. The king tried to persuade her to name the wedding-day. There was nothing for it but to go to her godmother again, who this time advised her to ask her father for a dress the colour of the moon.

The king, who could refuse her nothing, sent for the most skilful tailors in the land and ordered them to make a dress the colour of the moon and bring it to him within twenty-four hours. This they did, and the princess went to her ladies-in-waiting and nurse in great distress. The fairy Lilac, who knew everything, came to the

aid of the princess and said: 'If I'm not greatly mistaken, you will finally outwit your father if you ask him for a dress the colour of the sun, because he will never be able to find anyone who can do that.'

The princess went to her father and asked for the dress, and the besotted king took all the diamonds and rubies from his crown and gave orders for a dress to be made that was as glorious as the sun. When the dress was finished, it was so dazzling that all the tailors who worked on it had to close their eyes for fear of being blinded.

When the princess saw the dress she was horrified at what now lay ahead of her. Making the excuse that the brightness of the dress was hurting her eyes, she went to her room, where the fairy was waiting for her, more ashamed at the failure of her plan than she cared to admit. When the princess told her about the dress, she sighed and said: 'Oh, my child, we have no choice but to put your father's unworthy love to a terrible test. I know he intends to marry you, so we must ask him for something he won't be able to give you. Go and ask him for the skin of the donkey he loves so dearly, and which gives him so much money every morning!'

The princess, confident that her father would never sacrifice his beloved animal, went to him and asked for the donkey's skin. Although the king was shaken by her request, he ordered his servants to kill the poor donkey and take its skin to the princess. In despair, seeing no hope of avoiding her fate, she went to her god-mother again.

'Never mind, my child!' said the fairy, when she saw the girl's tear-streaked face. 'You are just going to have to run away. Wrap yourself in the donkey's skin, leave the palace, and walk as fast as your feet will carry you: the gods will look after you. I will see to it

that your clothes follow you everywhere; wherever you stop, a chest with your dresses and jewels in it will follow you underneath the ground. Here is my magic wand: take it with you, and when you need your clothes the chest will appear in front of your feet. Now hurry, you have very little time.'

The princess kissed her godmother and begged her not to desert her. Then she wrapped herself in the donkey-skin after first blackening her face with soot, and set out on her travels recognised by no one.

Her departure caused a great hubbub. The king, who had already ordered the wedding feast to be prepared, was beside himself. He ordered a hundred policemen and a thousand musketeers to go in search of his daughter, but her fairy protectress made her invisible to all pursuers. The princess travelled far and wide, searching everywhere for somewhere to stay and work to do, but although people gave her food out of charity, they found her so ugly and dirty that nobody wanted to give her a home. Finally, however, she reached a beautiful city at the gates of which was a farmstead. The farmer's wife needed a servant to tend her turkeys and clean out the pig sty, and when she set eyes on the wild-looking little creature dressed in an old animal-skin, she thought she would be just the person for the work. The princess accepted the offer gratefully, because she was tired of travelling. She was told to sleep in the farthest corner of the kitchen and during the first few days the servants teased her and made coarse jokes at her expense, because the donkey-skin made her look so dirty and ugly. Finally, however, they got used to her, and she did her job so well that the farmer's wife took her under her wing. The princess led the sheep and the turkeys to pasture with such skill that she seemed to have been born to the job, and everything she planted in the garden flourished.

One day she was sitting at the side of a clear pool when she suddenly caught sight of her reflection in the water, and the hideous donkey-skin covering her hair filled her with disgust. Ashamed, she quickly washed her face and hands so that they looked beautiful and fresh, but then she had to put on the donkey-skin again and go back to the farm. Happily for her, the following day was a holiday, and she tapped the ground with her magic wand to make the chest appear with all her clothes in it. She took out the dress that was the colour of the sky and put it on, and then combed her beautiful hair. Her little room was so tiny that she could not stretch out the skirt of the dress. She admired herself in the mirror and decided that from now on she would put on each of her dresses in turn on Sundays or holidays. When she did so, she would sigh, because the only creatures who saw her were the sheep and turkeys, who loved her anyway, even when she was wearing the donkey-skin.

One Sunday, the princess had put on her dress that was the colour of the sun, and was sitting in her room. The king's son stopped at the farm to rest on his way home from hunting. He was young and handsome, the apple of his parents' eye and adored by his subjects. After eating the simple meal that the farmer's wife offered him, he began to walk round the farmhouse. As he walked from room to room, he came to a dark corridor, at the end of which he saw a closed door. He bent down and put his eye to the keyhole, and to his amazement he saw a young girl dressed in wonderful clothes. She was so beautiful that he thought she must be a goddess, and he was too overawed to knock on the door.

Regretfully he left the dark little corridor, but decided he must find out who lived in the little room. He was told that one of the farm girls lived in it, and that the peasants called her 'Donkey-Skin' because of the way she dressed. They told him that nobody ever spoke to her, but the farmer's wife gave her shelter out of pity.

The prince wasn't really satisfied with this explanation, but he realized that it was all the peasants knew and it would be useless to ask them any more questions. He went back to his father's palace, already in love with the beautiful maiden he had glimpsed through the keyhole. He now wished he had opened her door and vowed that if he had another chance he would do so. But his love for the unknown girl caused a fever to rise in his blood, and he became seriously ill. The queen was in despair, because he was her only child; she promised all kinds of rewards to the best doctors in the kingdom if they could cure him, but no one was able to.

Finally the doctors came to the conclusion that the prince had something that was worrying him, and the queen begged her son to tell her the cause of his distress. She said that if he wanted to become king, his father would gladly step down and place the crown on his young head. If he was in love with some beautiful princess, no effort would be spared to win her hand. She begged the prince not to die, because her life and happiness depended on him.

The prince began to cry, but when he could speak he said in a feeble voice: 'Mother, I don't want my father's throne; I want him to live for many years and I will be his most loyal subject. As for being in love with a princess, I have never thought of marrying anyone, and anyway I would never disobey your wishes.'

'Oh, my son,' replied the queen, 'we will spare no expense to save your life, but my dearest boy, help your father and me by telling me what it is you want, so that we can try and obtain it for you.'

'All right, dear mother,' said the prince, 'I will obey you, for you and my father are the two people I love most. Mother, please ask Donkey-Skin to bake me a cake.'

The queen asked who Donkey-Skin might be. One of the officers replied: 'Your Majesty, Donkey-Skin is a funny, black-faced little person who lives in the farmhouse and looks after your turkeys.'

'All right then,' said the queen. 'My son must have eaten one of her cakes on his way back from hunting. Go and tell Donkey-Skin to bake him a cake as quickly as possible.'

A messenger was sent to the farmhouse with orders for Donkey-Skin to make a cake for the young prince.

Now she had seen the prince looking though the keyhole, and she had watched him from her little window as he departed. His image

119

often rose before her eyes and made her sigh with longing. So now, given the opportunity of doing something for him, she shut herself in her room, took off her donkey-skin, washed her face and hands, brushed her long blonde hair, put on a beautiful skirt and blouse made of silver thread, and started to make the cake. She used the purest flour and the freshest eggs and butter, and as she stirred the mixture a ring fell off her finger and into the bowl. When the cake was ready she wrapped herself in her donkey-skin and handed the cake to the messenger, asking him for news of the young prince's health. The messenger did not bother to reply, and hurried off with the cake to the palace.

The prince snatched the cake out of the messenger's hands and began to eat it so greedily that the doctors by his bedside shook their

heads disapprovingly. As he took one large mouthful, the prince almost choked on the ring, but he took it out of his mouth and his hunger disappeared when he saw the fine emerald mounted in a setting of pure gold to make a ring that was so delicate that it would only fit the slenderest finger in the world. He kissed the ring and put it under his pillow, taking it out from time to time and looking at it when no one was near.

He lay in bed wondering how he could find out who the ring belonged to. He was afraid that if he asked for Donkey-Skin she would not be allowed to come and see him, and he did not dare to tell anyone what he had seen through the keyhole for fear that he would be laughed at. All these thoughts bothered him and his fever began to rise again. The doctors told the queen that her son must be in love.

The king rushed to his son's bedside, and cried: 'My son, tell us the name of the girl you love, and we swear that we will give her to you, even if she is the lowest of our slave-girls.' The queen, hugging her son, agreed with the king. The prince, deeply moved by his parents' words, said: 'Mother and father, I would never marry someone against your will. But I would dearly love to meet the girl who is the owner of this ring, whoever she may be.' He took the ring out from under his pillow and showed it to them. 'It is so slender and delicate, I can't believe it belongs to a peasant-girl.'

The king and queen took the ring, examined it closely and came to the same conclusion. It should only belong to a girl of noble birth. So the king, after kissing his son and begging him to get better, went and gave orders for pipes, drums and trumpets to be sounded throughout the city, and ordered his heralds to tell all the maidens in the kingdom to come to the palace and try on the ring. The girl whose finger the ring fitted would be married to the prince.

First of all the princesses arrived, followed by the duchesses and baronesses, but try as they might, they could not squeeze the ring onto any of their fingers. Then came the working girls who, for all they were so pretty, all had fingers that were much too sturdy. The prince then asked for all the kitchen-maids and shepherdesses to be brought to him, and they were led in one by one, but they could not even get the ring on the tips of their thick red fingers.

The prince took his courage in both hands, and asked: 'Has the girl who baked me such a fine cake the other day tried on the ring?' Everyone began to laugh, and said she was too dirty and ugly to be brought to the palace. 'Nonsense, have her brought here at once!' ordered the king. 'I don't want it to be said that I have left anyone out.' So messengers were sent post-haste to fetch Donkey-Skin, who had heard the drums and cries of the heralds and could not understand the commotion that her ring was causing. Because she loved the prince and true love has no vanity, she was terrified in case some fine lady would try on the ring and make it fit.

When the messenger knocked on her door to fetch her to the palace, she was overjoyed, and quickly washed and combed her hair and put on her silver blouse and skirt made of silver thread embroid ered with fine emeralds. Then she wrapped herself in the donkey-skin and opened the door. The messengers, hooting with laughter, told her that the king wanted her to marry his son, and led her to the castle. When the prince saw her, he was horrified at her appearance and could not believe that this was the beautiful girl he had seen through the keyhole. Sad at having been deceived, he asked her: 'Are you the girl who sleeps in the little room at the end of the farmhouse corridor?'

'Yes, your Highness,' she replied.

'Then give me your hand,' he said, trembling and sighing deeply.

But then what a surprise! The king and queen and all the courtiers were amazed to see that Donkey-Skin had a delicate little white hand with slender fingers. The ring slid on her finger with perfect ease, and then, with a gentle movement, the princess let the donkey-skin fall to the ground.

She was so ravishingly lovely that the prince, feeble though he was, threw himself at her feet and kissed them, and the king and queen hugged and kissed her. The prince begged her to marry him at once, and she was just trying to thank him when the ceiling opened and the Fairy Lilac descended in a chariot made of leaves and lilac-blossoms. She told the king and queen Donkey-Skin's sad little life story.

The king and queen, delighted to learn that Donkey-Skin was in fact a real princess, hugged and kissed her again, and the prince's love for her increased a thousandfold.

The prince was so impatient to marry the princess that there was hardly time for all the preparations to be made. The princess made the one condition that she could not marry without the consent of her father, and an invitation was sent to him immediately. So on the wedding-day he arrived mounted on an elephant, with his new wife on another elephant behind him. The princess ran and kissed her father and stepmother, who had not been able to have a child of her own, and her father kissed her tenderly. Then the king and queen presented their son to him, and the wedding ceremony was begun. The happy bridal pair only had eyes for each other.

That same day the prince's father crowned his son king and placed him on the throne, and they lived happily ever after.

THE
FAIRIES

Once upon a time there was a widow who had two daughters. The elder daughter was the image of her mother both in character and appearance; they were both of them so disagreeable and haughty that no one could stand to be with them. The younger daughter, who was a faithful portrait of her honest and gentle father, was one of the most beautiful girls you have ever seen. Since people naturally like people who look like them, the old mother was extremely fond of her older daughter. She was very mean to the younger daughter and forced her to work from dawn till dusk.

One of the things the poor child had to do every day was to fetch water from a well that stood half a mile from their cottage. She had to carry the water back from the well in a large jug. One day, just as she was dipping the jug into the water, she saw an old woman standing by the well. 'My dear child, I am very thirsty. Do you think I could have some water out of your jug?' asked the old lady.

'Yes, of course,' said the good child, and after rinsing the jug out she dipped it into the coolest part of the well and held it up, supporting it so that the old woman could drink easily. When she had had enough, the old lady said: 'You are so beautiful and good, and so honest, that I cannot resist giving you a special gift,' (for the old lady was a fairy who had disguised herself as an old village-woman to test the goodness of the younger daughter). 'The gift I bestow on you,' continued the fairy, 'is that every word you utter will come out of your mouth either as a flower or as a precious stone.' When the child got back to the cottage, her mother scolded her for spending so long at the well. 'I am very sorry, mother,' said the younger daughter, 'for being so late.' And as she spoke, two red roses, two pearls and two huge diamonds came out of her mouth.

'What in the world do we have here?' cackled the mother in amazement. 'It looks as though the child's got diamonds and pearls in her mouth! How does this all come about, my daughter?' (This was the first time she had ever called her 'daughter'.)

The poor child innocently recounted everything that had happened, and a cascade of diamonds fell out of her mouth as she spoke. 'Goodness me,' said the old mother, 'I must send my older daughter there too. Look, Fenella, look what's coming out of your sister's mouth as she talks – wouldn't you like to have the same gift? All you have to do is to go to the fountain and when an old woman asks you for something to drink, just give it to her politely and courteously.'

'I don't see why I should go to the well to get water!' replied the older sister.

'Like it or not you *shall* go, and immediately!' ordered her mother. So she went on her way, grumbling, and took with her their most beautiful silver flask to carry the water in. No sooner had she arrived at the well than she saw a magnificently-dressed woman coming towards her out of the forest. It was the same fairy who had appeared to her sister, but this time she chose to take on the airs and graces of a princess in order to test how far the older sister's courtesy went. The beautiful woman asked for a drink of water.

'Do you think I'm here just to give you water?' said the older sister haughtily. 'I suppose you think I've brought my silver flask with the sole purpose of providing you with something to drink! Get your own drinking-water if you're so thirsty!'

'You are not particularly polite,' said the fairy, without getting angry. 'Well, well, since you're so disobliging, I'll give you the following gift: every time you say a word, either a snake or a toad will fall out of your mouth!'

When the mother saw her daughter approaching, she cried: 'Well, my girl!'

'Well, mother!' replied the older daughter and two vipers and two toads tumbled out of her mouth.

'Lord Almighty!' squawked the mother, 'what's this I see? It's her sister who's to blame! She'll pay for this!' and she chased the younger daughter with a broom. To escape being beaten, the poor child ran as fast as she could into the neighbouring forest.

The king's son, on his way back from hunting, saw her resting against a tree and asked her why she was sitting all alone and what she was crying about.

'Alas, my Lord, my mother has chased me out of the house.' As she spoke, five or six pearls and as many diamonds tumbled out of her mouth, and the king's son, fascinated, asked her where they came from. She told him about her adventure with the old woman and the gift she had received from her. The king's son, who had fallen in love with her at first sight, decided that this gift made her even more valuable and led her to his father's palace, where in due course they were married. As for the older sister, she became so hateful that her own mother chased her out of the house, and the unfortunate girl, after walking for many days without finding anyone to take her in, went into a corner of the forest to die.

LITTLE RED RIDING HOOD

Once upon a time there was a little village-girl, the prettiest you ever did see; her mother loved her dearly and her grandmother was devoted to her. Her grandmother made her a little red cape and hood, which suited her so well that everybody called her Little Red Riding Hood.

One day her mother baked some cakes and said to her: 'Go and see how your Grandma is, because someone told me she is sick. Take her a cake and this little pot of butter.'

Little Red Riding Hood set off straight away to see her grand-mother, who lived in another village. As she walked through a wood, she met a wolf, who would dearly have loved to gobble her up, but he didn't dare to because there were woodcutters nearby. Instead, he asked her where she was going, and the poor child, who didn't know how dangerous it is to stop and talk to a wolf, said to him:

'I'm going to see my Grandma, with this cake and a little pot of butter from my mother.'

'And does she live far from here?' asked the wolf.

'Oh, yes!' said Little Red Riding Hood. 'She lives over there beside the windmill, in the last house in the village.'

'Well fancy that!' said the wolf, 'I'm on my way to her house too; I'll go this way and you go that way, and we'll see who gets there first.' The wolf set off as fast as his legs would carry him on the path

that was the shortest route, and the little girl walked along the
longest path, amusing herself by gathering nuts, chasing after
butterflies, and picking bunches of pretty wild flowers. It didn't take
the wolf long to reach Grandma's house, and he knocked on the
door: 'Knock-knock.'

'Who's there?' called Grandma.

'It is your granddaughter, Little Red Riding Hood,' said the wolf in a high squeaky voice, 'bringing you a cake and a little pot of butter from my mother.'

Grandma, who was lying in bed because she felt a bit poorly, called out: 'Undo the hook and lift the latch.'

The wolf lifted the latch and opened the door. He pounced on the old lady and locked her in a cupboard. Then he put on one of the grandmother's nightgowns and a nightcap and climbed into her bed to lie in wait for Little Red Riding Hood. The little girl arrived a few minutes later.

'Knock-knock.'
'Who's there?'
Hearing the wolf's voice, Little Red Riding Hood was frightened at first – but then, thinking that her grandmother must have a bad cold, replied:

'It's your granddaughter, Little Red Riding Hood, bringing you a cake and a little pot of butter from my mother.'

The wolf replied, trying to make his voice a bit softer:

'Undo the hook and lift the latch.'

Little Red Riding Hood lifted the latch and opened the door. The wolf hid his head under the blankets and said: 'Put the cake and the little pot of butter on the table and come into bed with me.' Little Red Riding Hood was just about to climb into bed, but what she saw astonished her.

'Grandma, grandma, what big arms you've got!'
'All the better to hug you with, my child!'
'Grandma, grandma, what big legs you've got!'
'All the better to run with, my child!'
'Grandma, grandma, what big ears you've got!'
'All the better to hear you with, my child!'
'Grandma, grandma, what big eyes you've got!'

'All the better to see you with, my child!'
'Grandma, grandma, what big teeth you've got!'
'All the better to eat you with, my dear!' cried the wolf, and he leaped out of the bed and pounced on the little girl.

Little Red Riding Hood screamed! Just at that moment a woodcutter was passing the cottage. When he heard the scream he looked through the window. He was amazed to see a wolf wearing a nightgown and nightcap.

Then he saw Little Red Riding Hood. She was trying to run away, but the wicked wolf had grabbed the hood of her red cape.

The woodcutter ran to the door and rushed into the cottage. When the wolf saw him he jumped back in surprise and let go of Little Red Riding Hood. The woodcutter picked her up and put her safely behind the bed.

Then he lifted his axe and with one quick blow he killed the wicked wolf. The woodcutter turned to Little Red Riding Hood.

'Where is your grandmother?' he asked.

'I think the wolf has eaten her,' cried the poor little girl.

They heard noises coming from the cupboard. The woodcutter opened the cupboard door.

There was Little Red Riding Hood's grandmother sitting inside looking very pale and frightened.

Little Red Riding Hood hugged and kissed her grandmother in delight and gave her the cake and butter.

After that day Little Red Riding Hood never again wandered off the path in the woods, and she never talked to strangers when she was alone.